My Husband's Not Saved

By Clarissa Lee Kennerly

JUN 2012

Special Note

*C*larissa Lee Kennerly is married to Mark J. Kennerly. She is the niece of Mark D. Kennerly who is the pastor of Impact Christian Center and the author of <u>Extreme Preparation for Dating.</u>

This book is dedicated to my Lord and Savior Jesus Christ, who saved a wretch like me and allowed me to be a vessel for his words to come through. Thank you for never giving up on me . . . I praise you for your faithfulness. To my husband Mark J., who has always loved me for just being me, and who has allowed me to share our life with the world, to my children, Kylee & Sai, who are blessings from God and whose smiles remind me of his unconditional love, to my mother Julia, whose undying support and love has turned me into a better person, and last but not least to my pastors, Bishop Duane A. Ganther and Pastor Mark D. Kennerly, whose words have taught me more than they could ever know.

Table Of Contents

Introduction

J ust because your husband goes to church, doesn't make him saved. A lot of us settle for that. We think that is enough to make us happy because hey, he'll get the point someday. While going to church is important, it's just not adequate. We don't have to settle for a marriage that is less than what God has called it to be. Your husband is the head of your household; therefore he needs to be a man that desires the will of God for his family. As frustrating as it may seem right now, you *can* have that kind of husband. Maybe your husband is saved, but is not living like the mighty man of God that you know he can be. With God in it, satan does not have a chance and don't give him one. Throughout this book I share with you some of the things that I have gone through on my journey with my "unsaved husband". I share with you my most intimate and honest feelings through my journal entries before each chapter and explain what God revealed to me throughout them. What I ultimately found out from writing this book was that it wasn't about him, (it's not about him ladies) it's about us, and what we do with the knowledge that God gives us through His Word, and the lessons that He teaches us, which will in the long run make us closer to Him. Now He could have you in this situation for a number of reasons, or maybe you chose it for yourself. But whatever the case, God is in control, so remember that when you call out to him and cry "Lord, What should I do? My Husband's Not Saved"!

Is My Husband Saved?

One of the first things we should understand is whether or not our husbands are really saved. We could ask them, but do we really have to? We should be the closest person to our husbands. Our lives are intertwined and we should know if they are truly saved, regardless of what they say. I am not saying judge them, but know them. And in order to do that we must understand what it is to be saved.

I know that being saved takes more than saying "the prayer". I know that being a good man will not get you into heaven. I know that believing with all of your heart that Christ is Lord and keeping his commandments plays a huge role. But one day my husband made me second guess a little of what I already know, and learn a little bit more about him and his feelings about salvation.

I was a little nervous about telling Mark the title of this book. I guess I was afraid that I would offend him. But then I thought, why would I do that? I mean he isn't saved, is he? So I told him. Slowly. And he said, with a weird look on his face, "I'm saved". My response was "Oh". I was a little dumbfounded and a little confused. I mean I know that he walked down to the altar a time a two. I know he said the Prayer of Salvation, but does that really mean that he is saved? Another time he explained to me that he believed in God, that he believed in Jesus, that he said the prayer, he was good person, and took care of his family. He tried to keep the commandments, that he had his faults, but who didn't? He said that that has to count for something. And then he asked me if that was enough.

Church did nothing for him. He said that it would be as if I was not interested in soccer, yet he continuously asked me to go to matches. I didn't know what to say. I didn't know how to answer him. I needed to pray, but at that moment he was looking to me for an answer, and I gave him the best reply that I could at that time. I didn't want to be responsible for giving him an incorrect answer so I simply said, "I don't know". And I didn't. Does going to church really make that much of a difference? I wanted to be able to give him what he was looking for, the answers that he wanted, but I couldn't. So then I asked him what made him think that he was saved and he said it was because he said the prayer and that he believed. But is that all it takes? He then asked me the same question and I said it was the relationship that I had with God that made me confident that I was saved. Yes, I said the prayer too but then I changed my life, I became a new person, and God became my savior, my Father and my best friend. And I was not sure if you could be truly saved without the relationship...I just didn't know. So I asked a couple of strong Christians that I knew, and then, I asked God.

My Mom: *You have to. It's impossible. Because you have to have the spiritual relationship in order to do the will of God. Talking to him, praying, reading His Word because you would be doing it all through the flesh if not. Anyone can say a prayer but you have to have the spiritual relationship. You have to.*

Grandma: *You have to have the relationship with Him. Just being a good person is not good enough. Anyone can go to the altar but not be saved. You have to love him with all of your heart and you have to communicate with him because how else will He know you. In John 3:5 Jesus says, "Except a man be born again, he cannot see the kingdom of God". You must be born again, like a little child and when you are born again, you change. You get rid of all of your old ways and become a new person. Then you will want to have that relationship with God.* My Aunt: *Having a relationship with God is part of being saved. Take marriage for instance. How could you sustain your marriage if you didn't communicate? We are married to Christ. There is no way that you can claim to know someone if you do not talk to them. Once you are saved, you should want a relationship with Him. I knew a lady once who said "Oh Lord" and another person responded to her, you better call on someone who knows you!*

The Bible says in Matthew 7:23, *And then will I profess unto them, I never knew you: depart from me, ye that work iniquity.* Now in context this verse is talking about false teachers and prophets. But doesn't this also pertain to people who do not have a relationship with him and call on his name? Matthew 7:21 says *"Not every one that saith unto me, Lord,*

Lord, shall enter into the kingdom of heaven; but he that doeth the will of my Father which is in heaven."

If God doesn't know you, He *will* ask you to leave him. The word "know" means to be acquainted with, to identify, understand, experience, be familiar with, and to recognize. Think about that for a minute. We need to be acquainted with Him, able to identify Him, understand Him. . .experience Him. And you cannot do any of those things without having a relationship with Him. So yeah, my husband's not saved, but that doesn't mean that he will remain that way.

October 23rd

I *never wanted to be that wife who went to church with her kids without her husband. It wasn't like that in the beginning. In the beginning we went to church together and I loved it. Praising my God beside my husband was unexplainable. Then I became a mother and we were a real CHRISTIAN family. I kind of knew he wasn't that serious about God or the church for that matter, but in my mind I wanted to believe . . . I wanted to believe that my husband believed . . . but he didn't. The Bible says "Therefore judge nothing before the time, until the Lord come, who both will bring to light the hidden*

things of darkness, and will make manifest the coun-sels of the hearts: . . ." (I Corinthians 4:5) The word "manifest" means easily seen and God eventually did exactly what the scriptures said that He would. I truly saw and understood what was in my husband's heart. All of the feelings that he hid in darkness were brought to light. Now he won't have anything to do with church. He won't go and when I beg him to he begs me not to make him. The biggest problem is that I know that I have been called by God. I don't want to choose, but if I have to I'll be another thing that I never wanted to be . . . a divorced woman.

My Story

❖

Mark and I officially met in April of 1993. He was a skinny, scrawny, freshman with glasses that took up half of his face. I was an average junior with a low self-esteem who was still trying to find where I belonged. I had seen him around but never paid him any real attention and he had done the same. I didn't know then that he was going to make such an impact on my life.

Picture this . . . It's the 90's. My girlfriends and I were sitting at the lunch table checking out guys like typical 16 year olds do. My cousin turns to me and says, "Clarissa, you need a man". Being self conscious, I wanted nothing to do with having a "man". I had had a modest 4 boyfriends . . . with my first one being in the 7th grade. Compared to everyone else, I was far behind. I tried to play it off by insinuating that *I did not need a man*. But she wouldn't listen. "How about that one." she said and then pointed to Mark. It all seems like it happened in slow motion now. You know like one of those old made for TV movies where the girl and guy turn slowly and their eyes lock while cheesy theme music is playing in the background. But it was not like that at all. She pointed to Mark and I simply said, "He has nice eyes." Why did I say that, because like a flash she called him over to our table and set up a date. I was supposed to pick him up later that day, (I was the only one who had a car) and we were supposed to hang out. I took it as a joke and I thought to myself, you've got to be kidding. Several weeks later I found out that Mark had not taken it so lightly and waited for me to come pick him up while looking out of his front door for hours. He was hurt and disappointed.

Mark and I met a second time on the track team a month later. We exchanged numbers, officially started dating on June 7th, 1993, and the rest is history.

When Mark and I starting dating I was in a youth group called "Youths A Flame". This is where my journey with Christ first began. This is where I truly rededicated my life, received the Holy Ghost, and really fell in love with God. We had youth meetings every Wednesday night. Most of the time I went to hang out with friends but I always left with a new perspective on God's plan for my life. I was an active member. We went to concerts, put on plays, went to revivals and really sought the will of God for our teenage lives.

I always invited Mark to come to the meetings and he would. In the back of my mind I always knew that he was just coming to please me and I was OK with that. It would be later on that I would live to regret that decision.

Throughout our relationship, my relationship with God fluctuated. I was in that mode in which the only real time that I would spend talking to God was when I needed something from him. I had fallen in love with Mark and he came before everything else, including God.

Mark and I waited two years before we became intimate. It was when I was a freshman in college and I could tell that the distance in our relationship was growing. Before I left to go home that weekend I heard the voice of God. I believe it was the first time that I had actually heard that still small voice. I will never forget what He said to me. He told me to be careful. I automatically assumed that He was talking about the drive. I was so nervous that I took my time getting home. Now I know that He was talking about me letting down my guard, and becoming intimate with Mark. Even though I had put someone before God, He was still looking out for me. He knew that I was about to make a mistake.

Several weeks later Mark broke up with me. He said he didn't want to be with me anymore, he said I was smothering him. Crushed and depressed I turned to God. I started going back to the youth group during my summer vacation. I became close with God again. It was during that time that God told me about the plans He had for Mark and I. I then knew that we would get back together and a couple months later we did. And I once again I put God back on the shelf.

Mark and I broke up one more time before we got married. This time he moved to California to live with his uncle and pursue acting. Three thousand miles of distance couldn't keep us apart. We had sky-high phone bills, visited one another as much as we could and neither one of us could keep a relationship with another person because we always seemed to get in the way.

Mark's uncle was an aspiring actor who gave his life to Christ and became a minister. He went to church with his uncle's family on Sunday and went to various church functions. While Mark was doing that, I also had joined a new church and started a youth ministry. When we decided to get married we were in the same place spiritually. We were by no means perfect, and were not even giving a 60% effort towards doing the will of God. Nevertheless we loved Him, talked about Him and praised Him, and that was good enough for me to say, "I do." I loved Mark, he loved God and I envisioned us growing up in the ministry together. It would be perfect, and I would never have to be that woman who went to church without her husband because my husband had given his life to Christ . . . so I thought.

October 27th

❖

*M*y husband said something that scared me the other day. He said that when he thinks about God his mind always goes to the fact that God is not real, so he chooses not to think about him at all. I asked Him if he prayed to Him, or even thanked Him for his many blessings. His response was, "I don't know". I knew that if he didn't know, then the answer was no. It blows my mind how he can live day to day without speaking to God. God is my Savior, he is my Father, my best friend, my everything, and I cannot imagine living a life without Him and yet the man that I am married to does. It's not like I intended *to be married to a man that does not love or respect God. Some women choose that. They know how their husbands are before they marry them and they still say I do and then expect to change them later. That is not my story. We were both in the same place spiritually and somehow I moved forward and he moved backward . . . gosh, that's so hard to think about . . . I don't want to think about it . . . I just want it to change.*

Who Was I Kidding?

Deep down I knew that Mark wasn't as serious about the things of God as I wanted him to be. But I was a newlywed, I was young, in love and wasn't as serious about God as I knew that I should be but I figured we would change together. We went to church every Sunday and to almost every church function. We rarely went on Tuesdays for Bible Study and neither one of us did any act of service except Mark helped the men clean the church one Saturday a month. We were enjoying our carefree life and just going on Sundays to stay in favor with God. I was okay with this for about a year, but then the Holy

Spirit started to convict me and I wanted to do more. Talking to Mark about it was a lost cause. He didn't want to do anything else because he didn't feel the need to. There were several times when he would share with me that he didn't really feel anything at church and he didn't really pray. I just kept on hoping that the more he went, the more he would want to go. WRONG. Who was I kidding? Look at the example I was setting for him. I was living carefree all week and then wanted us to be more dedicated after being in church on Sundays. So I decided to change. I got a prayer partner who I prayed with every morning at 5:45 am. Next, I joined the Care Ministry. This was the ministry that greeted, prayed for, and called our first time attenders. We met every other Friday and discussed the ministry and the Word of God. I was definitely changing because of my involvement, but my husband was staying the same. I just couldn't bring myself to acknowledge it. I don't think I even brought it up to my prayer partner. I just pretended that nothing was going on, after all, we were very happy. Who was I to change things? I just thought that he was all right. That he was just praising God in his own way. He'd eventually come around.

One night at a Care Ministry meeting, one of the sisters was sharing about her past marriage and started to talk about the fact that her husband was not saved. When she finished she looked at me and told me how lucky I was that I had a husband who was saved. How lucky I was that I had a husband who loved God and that served him with all his heart. All I could do was shake my head yes but inside, my heart sank. I felt like everyone in the room was looking at me and shaking their head. It felt like they were all scolding me with their eyes and screaming the untruths about what she was saying. It was at that moment that I knew that everything was not all right. It was at that moment that I realized that my husband was going to church for me and his uncle but he was not going for himself. The truth was that he had no real desire to go and nothing was changing and I had been ignoring it for almost 3 years.

Needless to say, I wasn't surprised that Sunday in December when he said that he didn't want to go to church. He said he just didn't feel like it. By the end of the month he told me that he wouldn't be going back because he didn't feel comfortable. I didn't want to be that wife that takes her child to church while her husband stayed home and I confessed that to him. It was to no avail. So I simply stopped going to church as well.

Sunday after Sunday we sat in our living room. We watched TV, went shopping, slept in, took our daughter to the park and relaxed. I kept on telling myself that this was okay because I was spending time with my family. The longer we didn't go to church, the further away I drifted from God. A couple of saints from the church called to check on us and we said that we were fine and that we were just taking a break, but we weren't fine, at least I wasn't. I knew I was wrong and that I needed to just pick myself up and go back to church. But then fear set in. I was so afraid of so many things. I was afraid of what people would think. I was afraid of their questions. I was afraid of their pity. I was afraid of being that woman that I never wanted to be. I was afraid of losing my husband, losing the family and life that we had built together. A bigger problem arose when I began to become afraid of God. I wondered what He thought of me and wondered if I was still worthy to come into His house or to even utter His name. I wanted the best of both worlds so I began watching ministry on TV. That's how my grandmother was saved and she is one of the holiest people I know. Surely if it worked for her it could work for me. And it did work, for a while. But I didn't worship God and I didn't pray and pretty soon it just became more of a hassle than anything else, so I let that go too.

I was so ashamed, so I tried not to think about it. I made up every excuse in the book why it was okay for me not to go. I would tell myself that God honors marriage and that I was doing the will of God by staying with my husband. That is true. God does honor marriage, but He has to come first. It's not like Mark told me that he didn't want me to go to church. As a matter of fact, he encouraged it. When I would get depressed he would say things like, "You need to go to church". "You're a different person when you go to church". He was right, but I didn't want to go without him, so I stayed home.

October 29th

*It's not like I don't pray for him. I do, everyday.
I even had a breakthrough at church on Sunday
(once again alone). I believe that God showed me
that we (me and my husband) were going to be youth
leaders and marriage ministers when I was 18 and I
forgot. How quickly we forget the promises of God,
but now I remember and I believe it, I do. I need to
let go and let God and continue to pray, but man is it
hard. It is so hard to pray and to look for an inkling
of change and get nothing. My grandma always says
that no one said it was going to be easy. Boy, was she
right.*

But God . . .

Ihad not been to church in five months when we went to visit my family in Virginia. I was terrified to fly (always have been) and did not have God to call on. I mean I did have Him but I was too ashamed to ask Him for anything since I hadn't been to church in so long. I wasn't the same, and my pride would not allow me to ask Him for anything. The flight to Virginia was very hard for me. My husband slept on and off and I was counting every moment until we landed. It was horrible. Nevertheless we arrived safely and went on with our trip. We were only going to be there for 5 days but ended up staying for 2 weeks due to an unforeseen situation. What I saw as unfortunate, God saw as an opportunity. He did something for me that I will never forget.

When Mark and I decided to stay another week in Virginia we had to pay extra for our rental car and for our new airplane tickets. My mother did not have the internet and I needed to see our account so I asked her neighbor if I could use her computer. I knew very little about this woman except for she had been sick and God healed her and when He did, she became a new creation in Christ. After using her computer, I thanked her and was on my way out the door when she stopped me and asked me if she could pray with me. It struck me as kind of odd but I was always willing to pray. After we prayed, she looked at me and asked me why I wasn't giving God 100%. I was floored. How did she know that I wasn't giving God my all? She continued to talk to me and reveal things that only God would know and I became afraid. To this day I don't remember what her questions were but I know that they we dead on. I responded to them and I was on my way.

I went inside the house and went to find Mark. I told him everything she said and the next thing I knew she was out in the living room talking to my grandmother. I locked the bedroom door and I asked Mark what I should do. He told me to stay in the room, but I felt bad and went out to greet her. It was one of the best decisions that I ever made.

She prayed for me and spoke blessings into my life. For the first time ever I felt like God really wanted me, and that he was not going to let me go. He loved me so much that He was willing to go to those lengths to let me know. My life changed. It was at that moment that I decided with or without Mark I was going to live for God to the best of my ability. I no longer cared if I had to go to church by myself, that didn't matter to me anymore. It was God. And I knew that he would bring my husband along if I were faithful.

November 1st

I feel kind of guilty about what I said before... you know about the divorced thing in an earlier journal entry. I believe it was October 23rd. That is not God's will for my life. I am not supposed to be a divorced woman. To say that is to say that God cannot do what he says he can. I need to put my faith in Him and not think negative thoughts. I want to know in my heart that my husband will be a mighty man of God. I need to believe in things that are not true as though they are. Thank you God for my husband being a mighty warrior for your kingdom.

Shut Up and Pray

❖

When I started going back to church I was energized and I was excited. Kylee, my daughter, and I went almost every Sunday without Mark. There were times when my old feelings would try to resurface but God helped me to stay focused and on the right path. It was especially hard when the pastor would talk about husbands and how men were to be the head of the household. I would always wish that Mark were there. There was one time when they asked all of the married couples to turn and talk to one another and I had no one to talk to, I wasn't the only married woman there by herself, but I still felt all alone. It was during those times that I would ask Mark about coming back to church with me. He would tell me that he would come eventually and just to bear with him. I decided that it was wise for me just to bear with him and wait. Month by month I waited, occasionally asking the same question and he would give the same answer. I grew tired of waiting for him and even more tired of bearing with him. I felt like he was never going to come around and that I was going to be going to church alone forever. Don't get me wrong, I was prepared to do it, I just didn't want to. But I also realized that the more things I said to him, the more he withdrew, so I decided to just shut up and pray. I know it sounds easy, but it was not easy for an outspoken wife like me. There were plenty of times that I would steal away to my daughter's room to cry and pray. But when I came out of that room I remembered that I was a new crea- tion in Christ and could handle the rejection better.

I also began reading a book entitled <u>The Power of a Praying Wife</u> by Stomie Ormartian. If you haven't already read it, I would suggest it. It is a powerful book of support, love and more importantly God's Word. It helped me to see the bigger picture. That maybe it wasn't all about my husband, maybe it was about me. Maybe God was using this to test me, to teach me to pray more, to have undying faith, and to realize that with Him anything is possible, even bringing our husbands to Christ. It also helped me to pray for every area of my husband's life and that was special to me. I was doing more for my husband than any words I said to him ever could. I was interceding for him, talking to the Father on his behalf instead of mine and believing that God would honor my prayers. I was praying more for him then, than I had when he was going to church. I was finally doing something that I should have been doing all along.

November 2nd

I *have been trying to get Mark to come to a family fun day at church. As soon as I mentioned it he shut me down. I told him it was good for our marriage and that I didn't want to be the only married woman there without her spouse. (There's a special session for married couples) He told me to go and then when it gets to that point, leave. I prayed about it and asked God to help me choose the right time to ask him. He did. I asked him again today and he agreed. I praise You God . . .You are so faithful.*

He is Still Your Husband

Dear Mark,

Please forgive me for the things that I am about to say. I am ashamed and I apologize. This is not meant to hurt you in any way nor was it ever intended to. I had fallen into sin. If it weren't for the Holy Spirit's urging, I would keep this to myself. Thank you so much for your support and your understanding.

When Mark first stopped going to church, I was okay, because I had stopped going as well. But when I went back something had changed. I had lost respect for my husband. It wasn't so much that I showed it, but I certainly did feel it. Each week the pastor seemed to always hit on something that had to do with family. And there I was week after week, bringing my daughter, trying to do the will of God and there was my "so called" head of the household at home. I grew tired of making excuses for him in my mind and one day something just broke. It was my heart. I felt so alone. I still played the role as a "happy" wife, but I wasn't happy. I was learning so much, growing so much, and I couldn't share any of it with him. I tried to let him know what was going on in my life and every time he would let me down with his reactions. Here is an example of a typical conversation:

"Mark, Pastor spoke a good word today. He talked about faith and fear and that you can't have fear, if you have faith. I know he was speaking to me.

God has been working on me and I am so excited that He spoke through Pastor directly to me."

Mark would barely look away from the TV and would mumble, "Um hum." I got to the point that I didn't even want to talk to him about what God was doing in my life. That was hard. Here, the most important thing in my life, something that was becoming my life, couldn't be shared with my husband. I wanted to look up to him. I wanted him to lead our family and me. I wanted a man of God that I could respect, but my husband wasn't that person, therefore, I couldn't respect him. I lived with that for a while. Going through the motions and I kept my hurt and pain inside. Then one day I decided to talk to him about it.

"Mark", I said, "I'm afraid that we are falling apart." He looked at me shocked and retorted "Why would you say that dear?" "Well", I began, "I believe that God has plans for my life and I am going to start going to church more." "So" was his reply. "Since you're not going, I am afraid that we will have two different lives and morals. I mean look at Kylee. What if I believe one way on a subject because the Bible says so and you don't agree because you're not going to church? "We'll work it out," he said. "It's not that big of a deal." But it was a big deal to me. I wanted my husband and I to be on the same accord, Biblically. I didn't want my daughter to grow up confused. He seemed frustrated by the conversation so I left it alone but in my heart I was crying and in my mind I was thinking "Please God tell me that this is not my husband."

After I lost respect, I started committing adultery in my mind. Godly men, married or single was all I thought about. I thought about how my life would be if I was married to them instead of my husband. Soon the thoughts became fantasies. Full-blown fantasies. I would fantasize about how my "Godly" man and

I would pray together. How he would take care of any situation that arose by doing the will of God. How he would wake me up and say it's time to go to church. If I were upset, how he would use scripture to comfort me and if I started to backslide, he would be right there to help me get back to where I needed to be. We'd counsel unsaved married couples and I would never be at church by myself. I could stand from the pews and watch my husband serve God in any capacity. Whether he was a deacon, an elder or even a pastor, it didn't matter to me because I could look at my husband with respect and honor and oh how I would love him.

I didn't realize how deep in sin I was. I spent so much time envying what other women had that I lost focus and stopped praying. I allowed satan to take over my mind and at the same time, without me realizing it, destroy my marriage. I got to the point that if a single man of God looked at me, I would consider leaving my husband in the hopes of being with that single man, simply because he was saved. I Corinthians 7:15 says "But if the unbelieving (husband or wife) depart, let him depart." I was preparing to let Mark go, although he never said anything about leaving. As far as he was concerned we were still going to be married forever, but in my mind, we were already apart.

One Sunday my Pastor spoke about Proverbs 23:7 which says "As a man thinketh in his heart, so *is* he." That began to work on me. Look at what I was thinking about. Then he went on to talk about having faith and saying that we should speak things that were not true as though they were (Romans 4:17) and give God the glory. I really started thinking about that. The only thing that I wanted was for my husband to be a mighty man of God. I didn't want to lose him. I loved him. He was the father of my beautiful daughter and not only that, but I had made a commitment to him, in front of family, friends, and most importantly, in front of God. Had I lost my mind? Pastor then told us to turn to one another, basically partner up, and say, "You've got the victory." When I heard those words come out of my partner's mouth something inside of me changed. I began to cry and scream "Thank You Jesus" I started jumping up and down and praising Him. At that moment I knew what I had to do and I knew that if I did those things I would have the victory. I began to change my thought-life. I continued to think about how my life would be with a Godly man, but that man was Mark. I started thanking God everyday, out loud for my Godly husband. I started speaking out that Mark was a mighty man of God but he just didn't know it. I started speaking out that he was the head of my household and started praising God for him blessing me with a man that was a mighty warrior in His Kingdom. I was speaking things that weren't true as though they were true. And my respect for my husband came back. My appreciation for him came back. I saw him as a work in progress and I already knew the outcome. He was going to be a mighty man of God and I was just waiting patiently for him to realize that. But until he did, I continued to confess it.

It wasn't always easy. There were times when Mark would say things to me that would make me think that he really wasn't a mighty man of God, but then I would recognize it as a trick of the enemy and continued to confess what I knew to be true by faith.

Then one Sunday, Pastor talked about remembering the promises of God. And I began to remember. I remembered when I was going to church when I was about 17. I received a word from God. That word said that Mark and I were going to be youth ministers. That we would also be marriage counselors and that people would think that we were too young to counsel people in marriage but God would open their eyes to the gift that He had given us. When I remembered those promises, I knew, beyond a shadow of a doubt that Mark was coming back to Christ. He had to. God told me. He told me this before we were married, before we rededicated our lives, before we stopped going to church and before Mark wavered in his beliefs. From then on, it was easy for me to confess that Mark was a mighty man of God. If satan tried to tell me different I would reflect on God's promise for our lives and continue to confess it. Mark was still my husband and I wasn't going to allow satan to take him. *" Who can find a virtuous woman? for her price is far above rubies. The heart of her husband doth safely trust in her, so that he shall have no need of spoil. **She will do him good and not evil all the days of her life.**" Proverbs 31:10-12:*

November 5th

*T*he theme of women's weekend is "Remove, Restore and Renew". We are to write down what we want God to do for us so that we can share our testimonies afterwards. **Father God, I ask you to remove all doubt from my husband's mind about you and your kingdom. I ask that you restore him to the church, and that you renew his spirit so that he is a new creation in Christ. Thank you Lord. Amen.**

Remove, Renew, and Restore

❖

Women's weekend at our church consists of a lot of powerful events. There are 4 days of worship, the Word, fellowship, and of course God's presence all rolled into one. It goes from Thursday to Sunday and everyday there are different ministers preaching on a universal theme. It is all organized and funded by the women's ministry. There is also a family fun day on Saturday, which incorporates a marriage, single, and kid's seminar. My goal was to get Mark to come to at least one day of it . . . this is how the conversation went:

Attempt one: Mark, you know that I am singing in the women's choir this weekend. I would like it if you came to hear me sing.

Mark: Are you doing a solo?

Me: No.

Mark: Then I won't hear you sing, I'll hear the choir and I have heard them before.

A few days later . . .

Attempt two: Mark, I know that I am not singing a solo but it would mean a lot to me for you to come to see us sing. Don't you want to come to something I'm involved in?

Mark: I always come to stuff that you are involved in. You do not need me there. You'll be fine.

Several days later . . .

> *Attempt three: Mark, You don't have to come see me sing but I would really appreciate it if you came to the marriage seminar with me. I don't want to be the only woman there without her husband.*
>
> *Mark: Then don't go.*
>
> *Me: I have to, we might sing.*
>
> *Mark: So leave after you sing.*
>
> *Me: But I have to pay for a ticket and that would be a waste of money.*
>
> *Mark: No, it won't. Leave after you sing.*

A couple of days later I prayed something similar to this prayer:

Father God, help me. Give me the right time to ask my husband to come to church. Let me know when he will be in the right mood. Soften his heart

and give me the words and the time to ask. I thank
you in advance for the victory. In Jesus name I pray,
Amen.

The time was Sunday after church. I felt an urging
in my spirit. I walked up to him, sat down beside him
and this is how it went:

> **Attempt four: Mark, I need to talk to**
> **you. Please come with me to the marriage**
> **seminar on Saturday. It will mean a lot**
> **to me. I ... (Mark interrupts me)**
> **Mark: Okay, okay, I'll go.**
> **Me (silently): Thank you God, I**
> **love you and I praise you. You are so**
> **faithful.**

I wanted to scream and run around the room. I
wanted to shout and cry but I didn't. There would
be a time for that, but it wasn't then, not in front of
him. I said thank you quietly and did not make a big

deal of it, I didn't want to scare him. But when I got the chance I praised God until I couldn't praise Him anymore and even now as I am writing this I am still praising Him. He is awesome and loves us so much. I just can't contain it.

After I praised God and all of my excitement died down I thought about something. I realized that anyone can say that they are going to do something, but until they actually do it, it's just lip service. And that's when doubt set in. "What if he changes his mind?" There were so many factors. The night before the seminar I had planned a surprise birthday party for Mark. What if he was too tired to go in the morning? Also, I didn't have a babysitter for our daughter. What if he used that for an excuse? He would say that we have to tend to her and not be able to give the seminar our full attention. What if he got sick? (He has a habit of doing that before we are supposed to go somewhere.) What if . . . What if . . .

I had to stop all of those thoughts and the only way to do that was to pray. I prayed for God to take care of those situations, and He did. God even found me a babysitter and before I knew it, we were at church, together.

This was huge for me, and I was beaming. Here I was, at my Father's house, with my husband. This is something that I had been looking forward to, praying for, hoping for, for eleven months and God was doing it. He was really doing it and I knew that it just had to get better.

Our pastor preached the first part of the seminar to everyone. After it was over, we had lunch and fellowship. A lot of saints were coming to Mark and telling him how it was good to see him amongst other things but one saint asked if they would see him on Sunday, his response was yes. I just about jumped out of my skin. But I didn't show my excitement to Mark, I flashed him a smile and went on like nothing had happened but once again my spirit was jumping. I wanted Mark to go for himself, not for me, so I kept my cool.

Sunday morning we were in church. Me and my family and I knew that God was going to do something big. After the message we all stood for altar call and I could tell that Mark wanted to go. I knew that he did but I did not want to push him so I said nothing but I did pray. I prayed and asked God what I should do. Should I ask him if he wanted to go or not? I wasn't sure, but before I had to think about it another minute a member of the church asked him if he wanted to go, then she said that she would go with him and down the aisle they went. Excitement filled me but this time I couldn't hold it in. I was crying and praising God and giving him glory in every way I knew how. This was the day I had been waiting for, praying for; I just could not contain my happiness.

God had brought my husband back to church and I was grateful.

Mark rededicated his life on February 9th, 2003. It was one of the best days of my life. God changed me that day too and made my world complete with Him in the center. I was so prepared to start life with my renewed husband. Little did I know that the battle for Mark's soul was just beginning.

January 1st

❖

*L*ast night my husband almost gave a testimony. He was too shy to say in church but he told me. He said that he had lost a job and God gave him a new one, he had been kept safe despite his choice not to go to church for a while, he had a safe trip to Virginia and was back in church. I am elated. Just for Mark to acknowledge that God had done something for him was enough for me. He's changing. Praise God!

Joy

W hen my husband rededicated his life to Christ I was elated. The joy filled me from my head to my toes. I never thought that feeling would end. My husband started offering to go to church on Tuesday nights, seemed to be very interested in going to church on Sundays and going to Men's Fellowship. My joy was better than I had expected. I couldn't believe that God had actually done this for me. Well, it wasn't really for me . . . it was for His glory . . . but I was reaping the benefits. I couldn't have been happier until week by week, day by day, minute by minute Mark seemed to start losing interest until he eventually stopped going every Sunday, it was more like every other one. And as he lost interest, my joy started to fall until I completely felt like my prayers had gone unanswered. I became discouraged.

Joy is a funny thing—when things go our way, we have it, no question. But when things don't go our way, we lose it and that's it. That's not how God meant for it to be. When we ask for things from God, we are to have faith and rejoice in the fact that it is done. If it is not done when we want it, we are not supposed to give up hope and become discouraged. We are to continue to praise Him and thank Him and not lose that joy. Once I discovered that, I became happy once more. I know that my husband is a man of God and I am happy about it. I am joyous because my God gave him to me. Joy isn't only for the good times, it is for the bad also. God sees the beginning from the end. If we could do the same, think of how joyous we would always be.

February 1st

✧

*W*hat was I thinking? I stopped praying for him. I thought it was all done. Finished. I started praying for something else . . . (sigh). I should have known that as soon as my husband became saved that he would be under attack and more vulnerable. *I started praying less often because he was coming, I thought he changed. I can't help but believe that we are still at square 1.*

Square 2

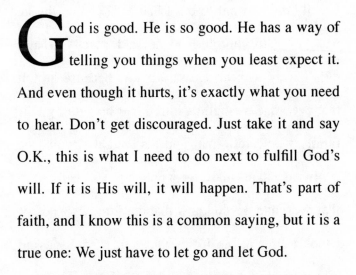

God is good. He is so good. He has a way of telling you things when you least expect it. And even though it hurts, it's exactly what you need to hear. Don't get discouraged. Just take it and say O.K., this is what I need to do next to fulfill God's will. If it is His will, it will happen. That's part of faith, and I know this is a common saying, but it is a true one: We just have to let go and let God.

One morning my husband said he wasn't going to church. I asked him why not and he said it was Super Bowl Sunday and he just wanted to stay home to avoid the hassle. I asked him if it was a hassle to wake up in the morning, or a hassle to hold his daughter in the morning and of course he said no. So I responded, "Yet it's a hassle to go to church to praise the one that allows all of that to happen." And his response was "I mean if you want to look at it like that, but it's a hassle to go to work, so it's just a hassle." Right then I knew he didn't have it. I really didn't want to but I had to ask him why he was going to church. And he said exactly what I didn't want to hear. He said it was because he felt that everyone was telling him that if he didn't go his family would fall apart and his daughter would be confused and his marriage would fail. He also said so that everyone would know that our family was okay. I took a breath, but I didn't lose it. I calmly asked him if he went to church for himself at all. He said he didn't know. I took a breath. He proceeded to tell me that he thinks he went to church just because he knew I was praying for him. This was an opportunity for me to start questioning God but instead, I started questioning myself. I couldn't believe that I had left him stranded like that. He accepted Christ as his Lord and Savior and I stopped praying because I assumed that he was fulfilled. He wasn't. I left my husband out there unprotected without a prayer to cling on. He was a brand new creation in Christ and I had allowed him to revert back to his own self. When he was first saved he was excited. He wanted to go to church on Tuesdays and on Sundays. And as time went by I eventually backed off of praying for him and started praying for other things. And as time went by he reverted back to his original self. Just going to church because it was the "right thing" to do. Then he said, "When you pray for me, don't just pray for me to go to church, pray for me to get that thing that you have, pray for it to hit me like bam. So that I will have that desire to go." I said, "Well you know you have to want it to receive it."

He answered, "I want it and I am still going to go to church, just not today."

I started racking my brain. I know that I prayed for God to change my husband's heart. I didn't just pray for him to come back to church. I was praying that he was a mighty man of God who didn't know it yet. I prayed powerful prayers, I know I did, but one thing that I didn't do, I didn't continue to fight the battle.

I made the decision that I would never stop praying for his spiritual life ever. Even when he does become that mighty man of God I will never stop because he will always be vulnerable to the tricks of the enemy. Our men need to be lifted up, always. I don't care how holy they are; lift them up because we have all fallen short of the glory of God. After all, **we are their wives**, their spiritual partners. We are one. Our prayers for our husbands carry more weight than anyone else's, even their mothers.

I am not at square 1, I am at square 2. The battle has just begun and I thank God that I am on the winning side.

February 29th

*T*oday I cried. I just want my family to be different. Why can't I have a husband who wants to go to church and praise God all the time? One who is so wrapped up in the things of God that his family has no choice but to follow him. **I want** to follow him as he follows God. This whole process seems like it's just playing with my emotions. One day he seems as though he is ready and is going to take that step and then other days it seems so hopeless. I feel like I can't take it. My emotions are on a roller coaster ride. I no longer want to get happy when he comes or when he says something profound *about God because for everything that he says that is encouraging, he says something equally discouraging. I have continued to confess that he is a mighty man of God with minimal results. This process seems impossible. Please God help me . . . I feel like I'm losing my faith again.*

My Walk

❖❖❖

I can tell that this chapter is going to be hard for me to write. Just now, just this moment, just this second God is teaching me something. He is telling me to look at my walk and myself and compare it to that of my husband's. He's saying do not look at the differences, look at the similarities and then see the truth. Breathe...I know, it's deep, I had to breathe too.

I Corinthians 7:14 says, *"For the unbelieving husband is sanctified by the wife . . ."* The Oxford Press Dictionary says that sanctify means "to make or declare holy; consecrate, to make legitimate or binding by religious sanction, and to be free from sin". Our unbelieving husbands are going to be made holy, legitimate, and free from sin, through Christ first and then us, their wives. What an awesome responsibility we have. And we can choose to do one of two things. We can either run from the responsibility and continue to feel the discomfort we feel from having unbelieving husbands or we can make the decision this very day that we are going to accept the responsibility and do everything that we can to ensure that our husbands are sanctified by us. It's our choice and it can be done because God does not put more on us than we can bear. We were put in this situation, and we can handle it.

Now that we have decided to accept this awesome responsibility to sanctify our husbands, you may be wondering how do we do it. We take a hard look at ourselves and don't make any excuses...because that's what our husbands are doing. They are watching our every move, everything that we say, and listening to every excuse that we make not to do the will of God. If we can do it, then why can't they? Then we get an attitude and get upset with them when they are just modeling our behavior. They are our mirror. I am not saying that if your husband is addicted to pornography that he is because of you, but maybe you are addicted to shopping, television, church activities, and all of these things are taking the place of you spending time with God. Let me give you an example.

My biggest problem right now is getting to church. I go on Sundays but on Tuesday and Friday nights I struggle. I always say that I am going to church but then I get tired and give all of these excuses. "I have worked all day and I am tired", or "I don't feel like it", and my personal favorite "I'll go next week". And then I have the nerve to get upset when my husband says those excuses when he doesn't want to go on

Sundays. It doesn't matter if you go every Sunday because we are not looking at the differences between our walks and our husbands' walks; we are looking at the similarities. Face it ladies, it's about us. We are showing them that church is important to us but it's not *that* important to us if we make up these excuses not to go. So why should it be so important to them? They need to see our passion and our consistency if that is what we want to see from them. Remember we will sanctify them, and how can that be if we are not sanctified ourselves.

Now maybe that's not you. Maybe you don't have any similarities between your walk and your husbands, *I Corinthians 7:16* says, *For what knowest thou, O wife, whether thou shalt save thy husband* . . . If there are absolutely no similarities after you have used a magnifying glass to look and prayed and asked God to reveal them to you then continue on, some sort of change will come and it will be for God's glory. And for those of us that see the similarities, pray and ask God to help you change them for the better. Pray for God to strengthen you in those areas and for your husband to notice the change. Don't get discouraged. It can and will be done. Think about the God that we serve. Think about his magnificence and his faithfulness. He is not going to leave us out to dry. He is teaching us something. We need to accept it, receive it, thank and praise him for it, and we will get the victory.

March 14th

*O*ne minute he says he is going to try to go to church and the next minute he gets all defensive about it. What is there to be all defensive about? It becomes an argument that I don't want to have. All I did was ask the question. There are times when it feels like I'd be better off by myself you know. I just want to serve God and it feels like he makes it difficult for me. Could he be holding me back?

He's Holding Me Back

There was a time when I had come to the decision that if my husband and God was laid out before me, and I had to make a choice, I would choose God. The choice for me then wasn't as easy as it would be now. No woman really wants to make that choice. We all want both. Sometimes it's hard to see women who have both when you don't. Jealousy and envy rears their ugly heads and we fall into sin. It can be a difficult thing if you let it. I am sure that we all have. It's ok. We just need to repent and ask God to help us to be proud of our husbands whether they are on the path or not and just to continue to pray for them. When I was in a youth group, there was a woman that had three kids. One my age, and two a few years older and she always went to church, with her kids, by herself. I think her husband might have come twice. Now, over ten years later I am told that he has finally taken his role as a true man of God and leader of his household. It is a beautiful, wonderful story. I am sure that her prayers have been answered. But I say that to say this, she never let her husband hold her back from doing what God had called her to do and I believe that because she was faithful, she was blessed.

You might be wondering what I mean by our husbands holding us back. I mean that you allow things dealing with your husband to get in the way of what God has called you to do. We have to get over the feelings of shame, and jealousy and go before God's throne and talk to him. We can't worry about what everyone else thinks. This struggle is bigger than them, it's bigger than us, and we have to <u>let go and let God</u> and not think about how long it is going to take. God is going to direct our paths because we don't know if our husbands will be saved (I Corinthians 7:16) but what we do know is that if God is in it, it doesn't matter what the ends going to be, he's going to get the victory which is extraordinary news for us. Regardless of their choice, we will continue to be blessed.

I often joke with myself that if I let this situation get so big that I ended up leaving Mark, God would replace me with someone who is faithful to him (Mark) and then Mark would become a mighty man of God and I would be alone and bitter because I hadn't been patient. Isn't that how it always happens? We are not patient and if we had waited just a little bit longer we would have gotten what we wanted, but we end up settling for something less than. That also pertains to the kingdom of God. Don't settle for less than what God has to give you. When you got married you entered into a covenant, not just with your husband, but also with God. We are not to throw that away in less there are cases of death, abandonment, or adultery. If your reasoning is that you believe that your husband is holding you back from what God has called you to do, you need to reexamine the situation. Is he forbidding you to go to church? Then what is stopping you? Is he forbidding you to read your Bible? Is he forbidding you to pray? These things do happen in extreme cases and if this is pertaining to you, no one can stop you from praying and seeking God in your mind. Continue to do that, God *will* bring you out. If you answer "No, but he makes it difficult for me." Then so what. We must pick up our cross and follow Christ. They made it difficult for him and he still followed God and so should we . . . regardless of our excuses. If your answers are anything like mine, just plain "no" to all of the above questions, then you should be ashamed of yourself. I am. We have been using our husbands as an excuse for our own shortcomings. Really think about this one, if we were with a godly man would we really change? Yes, the wife will be sanctified by her husband but in the end it is really our choice (I Corinthians 7:14). If you need your husband to do the will of God in order for you to do the will of God then there is a problem. Are our husbands holding us back? No way . . . we are doing this damage to ourselves.

March 11th

My husband is a good man. He is a fantastic husband, a phenomenal father, and a great provider. I feel like I would be in heaven if he realized that he was a mighty man of God and walked in it. When I look at other women whose husbands are in the church and doing the will of God, I wonder what their struggle is. I mean, when my husband does the will of God will my marriage be perfect? I don't think so. But somehow I think that it will be better. I feel like we would have a deeper connection, a spiritual connection. And it's not just about church, it's about him having that fulfilling relationship with God that would bring us closer together. Then we could talk about things on a spiritual level, and that would be wonderful. That would be really wonderful.

The Questions

I don't know about you, but my husband always seems to ask me questions about God that I can not answer. Every time he asks, I pray that God will give me the words to respond to him in a way that will satisfy him and make him understand why living for God is the only way to live. I don't have a problem with him asking me questions. It's kind of refreshing in a way because it means that he is thinking about it. And his questions are good questions. They make me want to go out and seek the answer but I never do. I think about it but then I get busy and move on to other things. I should stop, write down his questions and then seek wiser counsel to give him the answer. (Thank you God for that revelation!) He asks questions like: "How is there enough room in heaven or hell for everybody? Do you know how many people have lived on this earth?" or "How do you know that Christianity is right? Don't you think that the Buddhist thinks he's right or the Satanist thinks he's right?" It's hard to answer these questions without becoming defensive or having an argument but I try. Most of the time I end the conversation with "because I know." "Because I have a feeling deep down in the pit of my heart and my soul that tells me that God is real. I can feel his presence. Look at all of the things He has done for me. It is not a coincidence. He is real, Mark. I just know He is and nothing, nothing can make me change my mind."

Now that's all good and dandy for "believers" but for some men, who think logically and have to see it to believe it, that just does not suffice. Our unsaved husbands have never felt the presence of God so therefore it does not make sense to them. They are looking for a concrete answer and we have to give it to them. There are four basic things I have learned when it comes to the questions:

#1 Don't brush it off- Don't just brush the question off and act like he didn't ask it because you don't know the answer. If their salvation is important to us then we will take the question seriously no matter how silly or how illogical it may seem. Remember, they are watching us. If we make them feel like their questions are not important, then they will feel like it's not important for them to know the answer, or to change their lives.

#2 Find the answer- Write the question down. Tell your husband that you do not know the answer to his question at this time but you will find out for him. Then take the time to do that. If you are busy, come back to it later. Shut off the TV and get into the Word to find the answer. Do research on the internet (there is a lot of good information about the Bible and God on there, just be careful to weed out the bad), ask your pastor how he would answer that question, or ask a minister or an elder in the church. Don't give up until you find the answer and then tell your husband. Let him know that his questions are important to you and that you did not forget.

#3 Do not get frustrated- When our husbands counter what we say when we are trying to answer a question, do not get frustrated or defensive. It may seem as though he is attacking you and your beliefs and maybe he is, but think about it this way. He would not be asking the questions if he did not want to know the answer, and he only wants to know that answer because he is trying to figure this thing out. *Count it all joy!* That's good news. If he was not asking any questions at all then he's not thinking about it at all. Something that you have said or done has made an impact on him.

#4 Pray- Listen to his question and pray before you answer. I have a habit of praying while he's asking and then asking him to repeat the question. Ask God to give you the right words to say. Ask him to give you peace and to help you deal with the question in the way that he would have you to. Ask God to show you where you might find the answer. Ask him to give you an answer that will satisfy your husband until you find the answer. And ask him for the right time to bring the issue back up once you have found it. Trust him, He will. Think about what you will be doing when you are looking for these answers.

You will be studying and educating yourself on the things of God so if anyone else ever asks you, you will be prepared. Not only that but you will be growing spiritually. You will be spending more time in the word. Not only will you be answering your husbands questions but you will be studying to show yourself approved (II Timothy 2:15). How great is that!

April 11th

I *know how good God is. It often puzzles me that He could love measly old me as much as He does. I don't deserve His love, His forgiveness, or His grace. I am a sinner. Don't get me wrong, I try. I try to live by His Word but there are times that I feel like I don't try hard enough. I don't give it my all. It makes me wonder if being a Christian is as important to me as I say it is. I am constantly telling God that I love Him and that He is my life and all I want to do is please Him yet I fail Him. The unbelievable part is that He still loves me. No one can compete with that.*

Your Husband is a Sinner, Just Like You

"All Have Sinned and Fall Short of the Glory of God"- Romans 3:23

We have heard this popular verse. For most of us it gives us hope so that when we fall short we don't feel alone. We know from this verse that no one is perfect and that we all make mistakes. But isn't it interesting that when we become saved, we sometimes look down on people who are going through things and are sinning? Especially when it comes to sexual perversion, addictions and many other things. It is so easy for us to not only look at others that way but even easier for us to look at our husbands that way. I mean we are around them all the time. We know them more than anybody and we can hone in on their faults. Since we go to church and are saved and sanctified, it's okay for us to make mistakes, right? I mean since we are forgiven and all. God doesn't look at it that way. A sin is a sin, no matter who does it. Yes, we are forgiven because we ask for it and then we repent. But if we do not ask and we do not repent then we are in the same boat as everyone else. I don't care who we think we are. Even in the same boat as our husbands.

Mark and I had a spirit in our house. One that affected both of us. I realized what we needed to do to get rid of it. It got off of me, for the most part. I still struggled with it from time to time but I prayed, stayed away from it, and because of that it stayed away from me. But whenever it would get on Mark I would get really upset. So upset to the point that I forgot what a struggle it was for me. Imagine how much harder it would be for him. First of all, he didn't want it off of him as bad as I did because he didn't see a problem with it. Secondly, I was praying my way through. Somehow it made me think and even feel that I had the right to judge him. Instead of praying for him, I was looking down on him. He knew how I felt about the situation but I don't think he knew how I was feeling about him. I was wrong. I am no better than Mark is, I am just forgiven. And it is our duty to help our husbands with anything that they are struggling with, whether they know they are struggling or not. That's the hard part. It goes back to the familiar question of how do you help someone that doesn't want to be helped? You help them through prayer. Not only are we praying and confessing that our husbands are mighty men of God but we also need to be praying for the sins in their lives as well as pray for the sin in ours. We can't look down on them. We don't have the right.

I have heard on many occasions many people (including my husband) say that church folks think that they are better than everyone else. That they are the biggest hypocrites and are judgmental. No one wants to be around people like that. And we are our husbands biggest connection to the church, so we have to represent God's house well. If we are judgmental towards them, what do you think they will think about the life that we live? They won't want to be apart of it. No one wants to be treated like that nor should they be. How much trouble would we be in if God did not look beyond our faults? Scary, huh?

April 25th

❖

*M*y husband was looking at the memoirs for this book and he asked me why my book was all about him. I answered him by saying that it was not about him, it was about me. When I started writing it, I hadn't intended it being about me per se, but through it all I have realized that that's whom it's really all about. It's really all about me. It's about how I handle the situation that I am in and how I am growing and changing because of it. I was talking to God about two weeks ago and I recognized that in the end it is just he and I. When I stand before Him in judgment it will not have anything to do with *anyone else but me and what I did to serve Him. In the end it's my relationship with God that is going to make the difference in my life. And I like that, I really, really like that.*

It's All About Me

I know that throughout this book so far it's been
my husband this and our husband that, and I know
that the title of it is "My Husband's Not Saved", but
as I am writing it, I am realizing that it is more about
us, the wives, than it is about our husbands. Yes,
most of us reading this have a commonality in that
our husbands have not stepped into the things that
God has prepared for them but I believe that God
is teaching us not only how to handle it, but how to
grow as woman of God. God knew that we would be
in this situation. He knew that we would feel hurt,
lonely, and yearn for our husbands to come in line

with his Word. But He also knew how we would change through this. How our relationship with Him would become deeper and more fulfilling. How He would be the man in our lives, our confidant, and our defender. For some reason we needed this and He is going to get the glory through all of it. It all makes sense, doesn't it? God takes us through for a reason and even though we don't see it now, later we will, and then we will be all the happier that He did.

Have you ever been frustrated with God? You prayed for something and it didn't go your way. But then, later, you were happy that it didn't go your way because if it had, it would have been an even bigger disaster. I know I have. Wouldn't it be great just to trust Him all of the time and to not worry about anything? That's what we are commanded to do. I know it's easier said than done but wouldn't it make our life so much easier? Sometimes I feel like God is saying, "When will my child finally get it? I am looking out for your best interest and mine. I have proven myself to you time and time again and yet you still question me. When are you going to get it?" Once our husbands become saved then it will be something else, won't it? Or will we finally say to our souls that we will never doubt God again? That's why I say that it is really about us. God is working on our behalf and even though it doesn't seem like it we have got to let it go and let God work on us.

If Jesus returned right now, we could not blame our lack of prayer or our church attendance on our husbands because it's not about them. It's about us. God is molding us ladies. He is taking us through and when you go through something you eventually come out of it and we will. You are going to come out of it a more godly, faithful and spiritual women. You are going to come out of this with a stronger relationship with God. You are going to come out of it exactly where God wants you to be and where

He wants you to be is where we want to be. I know it's not easy, nobody said it was going to be, but He is our father. And there's nothing like a relationship between a father and his little girls.

April 27th

❖

*L*ast night I asked Mark if he wanted to go to church with me. He said no. So I said you should go because you are taking a chance. He then became defensive. He asked how he was taking a chance. I responded that he was taking a chance of missing something that could be said that could change his life. He said something might not be said that would change his life. I agreed and added that this was the reason that he was taking a chance. I said that if Jesus came back before he took that chance he would be sorry. Now I didn't say it vindic-tively . . . I said it as a matter of speaking. He started *accusing me of convicting him. I said it wasn't me, it was the Holy Spirit. He said no, that I was convicting him and I thought I was better than him. He further exclaimed that I didn't always go to church on Tuesdays and I had no right to convict him. I apologized to him and said that was not my intention. At the time I didn't think I had done anything wrong. Right now as I am writing this I guess I was a little teeny weenie bit out of line but not much. I know it was the Holy Spirit and it made me happy. He was bit uncomfortable but not angry. I could tell it was making him think. Praise God for thinking! "For as he thinketh in his heart, so is he" (Proverbs 23:7).*

Say What?

My pastor is very keen on words. He doesn't like to hear anything negative nor does he allow anything negative to be put on him. Even if it's an expression like "You're driving me crazy". And if you do your research you'll find out that he is right. God used words to bring the world into existence which shows you their strength. The tongue is a powerful thing. There are several Bible scriptures that denote that. Therefore we have to be very careful about the things we say and the things that we do not say.

Oh don't act like you don't ever say anything bad or negative about your husband. Especially when you are in a mood and he can't do anything right and the fact that he still is not going to church doesn't help things either, as a matter of fact, it makes things worse. We could be upset about the fact that he didn't wash the dishes and those thoughts creep into our head that go something like this: "If he was a godly man he would do this, or he would do that because he would love the Lord and be living a lifestyle to try to please God which would include him loving me just as Christ loved the church (Ephesians 5:25). After all, that's what the Word says. And if he were treating me like a treasure, those dishes would have been done." And if we are not careful, we might speak some of those negative things into existence. By thinking that and saying that we are still speaking the facts as they are and not as they will be. We are abating the fact that our husbands are not saved and by thinking that way or speaking that, we are binding them to that when we want the exact opposite.

The most powerful thing that Mark and I learned in pre-marital counseling was not to share what happens in our marriage. Of course the great and wonderful things are fair game. Who doesn't want to hear good news? I'm talking about the hurts and disagreements that everyone faces as a married couple. My pastor believes that we all need at least one or two mature Christian couples to turn to and tell our difficulties in marriage to and I am inclined to agree. These couples should speak life into in your marriage and give good, sound, godly advice, but I am talking specifically about our friends and family who are not mature Christians, not saved and not married. These are the people you need to steer clear of when these issues come up. To continually speak that negative thing is to not only relive the hurt over and over again but it is also keeping that thing around in the atmosphere. And when our friends and family members hear it, give their opinion and then tell someone else, they are speaking it into the atmosphere and then the person they tell tells someone else and the cycle continues. We don't want to give anything dominion in our lives, let alone allow others to do it. We need to learn how to tell God, those seasoned couples and no one else, especially when it comes to our marriage.

"You mean to tell me that I should not tell my girlfriends when my husband hurts me, sometimes I just need someone to talk to". I'm saying that we have to be careful who we talk to and even more careful about what we say.

When I say we have to be careful about what we say, that's exactly what I mean. The Bible demands it. Proverbs 12:18 (NIV) says, *"reckless words pierce like a sword, but the tongue of the wise brings healing"*. We have to be wise with our words, especially since we are trying to save our husbands. We must be wise so that they can be healed from whatever it is that's ailing them and causing them to stay away from God's will.

Psalms 64:3 (NIV) says, *"that they sharpen their tongues like swords and aim their words like deadly arrows"*. This verse is about an enemy. In our case, when we use negative words that is what we are becoming, our husbands' enemy. Words in that passage are being compared to deadly arrows. What does that tell you? I'll tell you what it tells me. It tells me that the old saying stick and stones may break your bones but words will never hurt you is not true. Have you ever aimed your words at your husband? Think about it. Think about the last big argument you had. Did you say anything that was aimed directly at your husband that would hurt? Have you ever? In situations like that we need to practice silence. Proverbs 10:19 (NIV) says, *"When words are many, sin is not absent, but he who holds his tongue is wise."* When *"words are many"* is what struck me. When I am arguing with my husband it seems as though I always have to have the last word, which makes my words many, and sin present. But to hold our tongue is wise and God will bless us for it. There are many other scriptures that support us holding our tongue in those situations. The Word of God also tells us the consequences for not holding it. Proverbs 21:23 (NIV) says, *"He who guards his mouth and his tongue keeps himself from calamity."* How many times have you said to yourself in hindsight that you just should not have said anything? I know I have a lot. And this is not just with our husbands but in other situations as well. This is not to say that you should let people run over you but there are things that are better left unsaid. Whenever I question it, I pray and God leads me, just like He will lead you.

A very wise woman spoke at a marriage seminar. She had been married 30 plus years and she told the women to be careful with what we say. She said that she doesn't know how many times she had to go into the bathroom, shut the door and pray with tears streaming down her face to keep her from saying some inappropriate things to her husband. I know what you're thinking. Probably the same thing I was thinking . . . but what if they are wrong. Don't they need to be told that? And why do we (women) always have to make the sacrifices? But then I was told that God blesses obedience. He will take care of it for us and will make the situation so much better. Several women have shared with me that when they go to God with their concerns that He will cause their husbands to see their errors or cause the women to see their own mistakes. Either way, it's better than speaking things you will later regret.

I used to have a problem with that. When I would get angry with Mark I would think of every hurtful thing possible to say to him. Finally he got tired of it and told me that I was not going to disrespect him like that any longer. He said it in a way that made me want to do nothing but respect him . . . (*you know what I mean ladies, in a stern way that makes you say dang, that's my man*). Words hurt and as women we should know that. Often it opens wounds that take time to heal. And even though our husbands may not say it, they hurt them too. Remember, they are watching us to not only see what we do, but also to hear what we say.

April 28ᵗʰ

*L*ast night a friend expressed the sentiment
that it shouldn't matter if my husband went
to church or not, at least I had one. Coming from a
single, Christian point of view, it made me think. Is it
better to have a husband just for the sake of having
one, or should we wait for the one that God has for
us? I think we all know the answer to that question.
Don't get me wrong . . . my husband is a phenomenal
man and I would not trade him in, but if I had waited
for him to step into the will of God first, things would
have been different, right? Would I have married
him? Or would he have married someone else and

still have me waiting in the wings? Either way I guess

it doesn't matter now. I am happy to be married to my

husband and I wouldn't have it any other way . . .

Don't Rush

When my husband went up to give his life to God in November I thought that was it. I had never felt joy like that before. I was so excited that I told everyone, saved or not. I praised God for days and days after that and then it wore off. Not me praising God, but my husband's fire for God. With each passing day it died a little more until it was finally quenched. I am not going to lie, it sucked. (Mom I know you hate that word, please forgive me, but that's how it felt) And it still does. I prayed for eleven months, wasn't that long enough? I instantly became aware that it wasn't. And not only did I realize that but I lost my desire to pray for him. I felt like it wouldn't make a difference. After all, Mark would ultimately have to make up his own mind. What was I wasting my time for?

I know that when you are in your mess, it feels like you are the only one going through. It feels like your cares and worries and bigger than everyone else's and that you and God are the only two in the world. Of course He is going to answer your prayers because you love Him, you are faithful to Him, and His Word says to ask and you shall receive (Matthew 7:8). I felt this way as well. That's just how it is or how it was until I realized that I was not the only one. I was in a church filled with people who needed their prayers answered and they had been praying a lot longer than me. Not only had they been praying for way more than eleven months, but they were also dedicated intercessors. Early morning prayers, late night prayer, overnight prayer and they were still waiting on their blessing. What was I rushing for?

I know. You want what you want, when you want it, and how you want it. Then you think of all of these reasons why your prayers should be answered. These were some of mine: You will have another person in the kingdom, I will be a stronger Christian with my husband standing behind me, helping me and encouraging me, my family life will be so much better with my husband being led by You, my marriage will have that spiritual side that it is missing. What could be so bad about my prayer being answered? In our mind, nothing . . . but our thoughts are not God's thoughts and our ways are not his ways (Isaiah 55:8-9). The only thing that we know is that He knows best and we have to have faith in that.

Have you ever rushed to do something and it turned out to be a disaster because you couldn't wait? This has happened to me several times. Let me give you an example. Mark and I didn't have the best credit and we needed to buy a car. I was pregnant with Kylee and we only had one vehicle. I was due in about 2 weeks. So we went to a dealership that catered to people that did not have the best credit, and bought a car. We did not consult God, we did not look around, we just bought the car because we felt that we needed it ASAP. Mistake. This car was worth 5x less than what we paid for it, which would make it almost impossible to trade in without the loan being paid off. Furthermore, a week later, Mark's friend told him that he knew people who would have given us a good deal despite the credit yet we were already locked into this horrible deal. You learn from your mistakes, and I learned not to rush into anything like that again. But isn't that how it is with God? We know that He knows what is best for us in the end, yet we want to rush everything to suit us and it ends up getting us into trouble. We rush to get married, to get divorced, to take a job that pays more money or to quit a job that seems to be going no where but if we had stayed in the situation just a little bit longer and waited on God, we would have been blessed with a better outcome. In the long run, it's better not to rush. Continue to pray, God's got your back and He has all the time in the world, literally.

May 2nd

❖

*M*ark's changing. I know he is. He has expressed several different things that show me that he is continuously thinking about God and church. The other night, I actually had the opportunity to show him how to pray! How awesome is that? He **is** going through something though . . . but I did pray that God take Mark through whatever he needed to, to help him realize God's will for his life and touch him so that he can't help but call out and praise God's holy name. And even though he is still not keen on going to church, I know the Holy Spirit is working on him and I know that his day of salvation *is not far away, no matter what he says, his day of salvation is not far away.*

Facing the Impossible

Does it ever feel like it's not going to happen? You have prayed so many nights and continued to confess your husbands salvation and he just seems to drift further and further away? I feel like that from time to time. Just when I get my hopes up, he says something or does something that causes him to fall. The whole issue is hope. Are we really supposed to be hoping? Does faith include hope, or is it something that you have to know? The Bible says that faith is the substance of things hoped for, the evidence of things not seen. (Hebrews 11:1) Not seeing is hard; I know it is hard for me. But nothing worth having is hardly ever easy.

My pastor started a series at our church about doing the impossible. It's amazing how God will give the word that you need to hear. I have rarely been in a service that does not pertain to me on some level, but this series was made for me.

I had gotten into the habit of thinking that Mark wasn't going to change and that I was meant to be with someone else. Although I had been through all of this craziness months before when I wrote "He is still your husband", I still thought that maybe I was supposed to be with someone else being that Mark was never going to change. I felt like it was impossible. I had been through so many ups and downs with him (many of which you have read about) that I finally deemed the situation, impossible. Yes, I love God and He has never failed me nor let me down, but I was tired. Tired of hoping, tired of my emotions being played like a yo-yo. I wanted answers. I wanted to know whether Mark was really going to dedicate his life to Christ or was I just wasting my time. It hurt. I was frustrated and kind of in disbelief that it was over and that I had lost this battle. Maybe God didn't want Mark to be saved. Maybe Mark had not been called to the ministry and he was just one of those people who would never find salvation. Maybe. I mean why else hadn't Mark given his life to Christ? I have prayed, I have called out to God, I have confessed it and I have believed it and yet he still was not saved. What was the deal? Was this an impossible request? I mean God did give us free will. The suspense was killing me and I didn't know what to do.

Bright and early Sunday morning, my pastor takes the pulpit. He gives his sermon a title as he always does and this one was entitled "A Passion for the Impossible." There are tons of stories in the Bible when it seems as though things are hopeless and just before it seems as though there is no way out of it, God intervenes. Look at Daniel and the Lion's Den, Meshach, Shadrach and Abendigo, Job, need I go on. And we all know and love these stories, but my pastor didn't tell a story of what God could do, he showed us what we needed to do if we wanted God to do the impossible for us.

I am sure that you know what I am going to say is the most important thing and you know this because it's true. It's faith. Unmovable faith. I struggle with that. For some reason I believe that God is going to do for any and everyone else that I pray for, just not me. I guess I don't feel like I'm worthy, I don't know. But I learned that day that I have to believe the thing that is impossible, is possible, in essence, have faith. The Bible says in Matthew 21:22 *"And all things, whatsoever ye shall ask in prayer, believing, ye shall receive."* If a person is unwilling to believe that it is

140

possible, then there's no faith. But if you believe and continue to believe, your impossibility will become a reality.

I know, it seems like a long time. At least that's how I was feeling but then my pastor used this fabulous analogy. He said that sometimes God wants you to stay in your situation for a while. He said that gold does not become 24 carat until it sits in the fire for a long time. People love 24 carat gold because it is more valuable, and it is more valuable because it is so pure. Since it stays in the fire longer, more of its impurities have been burned off and it is pliable, bendable, softer, and it can conform easier to the shape that the designer has planned for. Now think about us as the gold. God wants get all impurities off of us. And even though we may not completely understand how this situation is helping him do it, it is being done. He is making us more pliable, bendable, and softer so that he can conform us into the wives that we need to be for our husbands, and more importantly, so he can mold us into the women that He wants us to be, for His kingdom. My pastor ended his sermon by saying that sometimes you don't understand what it is like to be out of a situation, until you have really been in one. And I couldn't agree more.

All of this really applies to our marriages. If God is using this to make us more pure and to show us how to appreciate our men of God then I am all for it. If God is using this to teach us to have unmovable faith then I am ready to be patient. I am ready to learn, I am ready to change, I am ready to be everything that he has called me to be and I praise him for it. I believe that God is making me into the woman that I need to be to be with my mighty man of God! I believe my husband will be all that God has for him and it's not impossible, it's definite.

May 6th

Mark's job has been requiring him to work overtime. 16 hours to be exact. My daughter and I have been spending a lot of time together and sometimes I get lonely. Kylee is two. Sometimes I just need some adult conversation. I teach 8th graders all day, pick up Kylee and we come home to an empty house, and I miss him. I know he comes home eventually but when he does he is tired, and when I wake up he's gone, and I miss him. They say this overtime will last a couple of months and I know I'll be okay but it's hard. Once Mark asked me if a woman that goes church could have a husband that didn't *and them still have a good marriage. I thought to myself, well we have a good one, right? The more I miss him the more I realize that we do, and I am thankful to God for that. I know Mark is a mighty man of God and I know I say that a lot but that's only because it's true. And because we have a deep relationship without him being in the will of God makes me realize how much of an influence I am on him and how much more powerful our marriage will become once he commits. Then I can share with him and he can share with me and we will become one like we have never been before. I know that day is coming but until it does, I will forever be grateful unto you God for giving him to me. There are spiritual parts to our relationship that are missing, but the parts that are there, make this whole process worth the wait.*

Sometimes, it gets lonely . . .

❖❖

One day my husband is going to be encouraging me to go to church. One day, my husband is going to encourage me to pray in my time of need, he will pray for me and with me. One day, we will hold hands and praise God together and discuss His faithfulness and worship His holy name. One day . . . I know it's true, but until then, sometimes, it feels lonely.

Loneliness is the opposite of companionship. And in the kingdom of God, fellowship with your brothers and sisters in Christ is important. We are not to be unequally yoked (II Corinthians 6:14) and the Bible also says that iron sharpens iron (Proverbs 27:17). In other words we should share our most intimate times with people who believe the same as us and be so careful to not let our brothers and sisters go astray. With all of that being said, how do we do this when our husbands are not saved? I mean we are one with our husbands. We are called to be their helpmate and the most intimate conversations and most intimate times are spent with them. Amos 3:3 says, "Can two walk together, except they be agreed?" So how do we walk together with them? How do we keep their iron from sharpening ours and when we do, how do we keep from feeling so lonely in our marriage when it comes to the most important thing in our lives, God?

One way that we can keep from feeling lonely is to develop a close friendship with God. We can tell Him anything. And we can share our feelings with Him about the way that we feel about living for Him.

We can celebrate everything that He is and what He means to us with Him. We can also share with Him our disappointments and our hurts. A lot of times as women we have the need to get some things off of our chest, and if it is a conversation that is too taboo to talk about with our husbands, we can talk about it with our heavenly Father. Not only is He our Father, but He is also our friend and our confidant. He will give us the feedback that our husbands or anyone else cannot.

Another way to overcome this feeling is to make the decision that you will not be lonely. Decide that you do not have to share this area of your life with your husband if he is not willing to receive it, and be comfortable with that. Now I'm not saying to never tell your husband of what God has done for you and your family but you have to be willing to deal with whatever response he gives you. Don't turn it into an argument. Turn it into a prayer. Ask God to soften your husband's heart so he can view the blessings of God the way you do. And until he does, ask God to give you the strength and the patience to deal with the situation. Talk to Him, He truly does care.

There are certain things about my walk with God that I do share with Mark, and some I do not because I don't think he'll understand. Of the things I do share, his response is basically the same, "Oh really", but I know that he hears me. The things that I do not share are not a secret, but I don't know how he will respond or if he will respond at all. It is those times when I talk to God about it or even other believers. It is nice to share those experiences with people who can relate and have been through the same thing. Even if they haven't, they understand it, and that helps to keep you from feeling so lonely.

Psalms 62:1-2 & 5 says, *Truly my soul waited upon God: from him cometh my salvation. He only is my rock and my salvation; he is my defense; I shall not be greatly moved . . . My soul, wait thou only upon God; for my expectation is from him.* God is the only one providing our salvation; He is our rock and our strength. He is the only one that can truly defend us and the only one that we can truly depend on. He is always with us, how can we ever feel lonely? As long as we have Him, and talk to Him, we can and will overcome that feeling of loneliness. Just think, the more we talk to God the closer He gets to us, and who doesn't want that close, deep relationship with God? I know I do. Take this opportunity to get it and get rid of your lonely feeling at the same time.

May 10th

✦

*Y*esterday was Mother's Day and my pastor
taught the women's Sunday school class. It was
cool. We talked about things that women should do
for their husbands and one of the women proceeded
to talk about us getting caught up in the little things
(like our husbands not going to church) instead of
us understanding our roles. She basically said that
of course we want them to come but we should not
stop fulfilling our roles as the helpmate just because
he doesn't go to church. We still have to do our part.
After that, church started and I was very happy to
see that my husband came. We sat in church together,

holding hands. I can't tell you what that did for me. Gosh I miss him when he doesn't come. It was nice. And you know what's even better than that, it's just a glimpse of what's to come.

A Glimpse of What's to Come

G od takes us through many different situations to teach us, and to mold us, in order to prepare us for things that are coming in our future. He tests us to see if we are ready, and puts trials and tribulations in our path to mold us into the individuals that we need to become in order to fulfill His plan for our lives. It could be really big things, or really small things but nevertheless, they are things that we don't understand, and don't need to because in the end it will all make sense.

God sees the beginning from the end. How would you like to be able to do that? It would make life so much easier for us. If we knew what the end result would be, we would be willing to go through all of the trials and tribulations without reservation. A perfect example is when I had my daughter.

Being pregnant was no picnic for me. I didn't have morning sickness and I wasn't on bed rest, I just had these terrible headaches and to tell you the truth, I just flat out didn't like it. Nine months of that can drive you crazy and there were times when I felt that if I didn't have God, I would have been. I went into labor about 11:00 am on a Sunday morning and gave birth at 12:11am Monday morning. It was interesting to say the least, and very painful I might add. Through the process though, I wanted to give up, I demanded that my husband take me home. At one point I even stopped pushing, stopped trying, I just wanted the pain to end. But the result of it all was this precious baby girl that I held in my arms. This beautiful angel whom I had never met, but loved her more than I had ever loved anyone in my life. And as much as I hated being pregnant, and as hard as my labor was, I would have gone through it all again just to have her, just to hold her, just to love her. If I would have known how I would have felt after everything was over with, I would have rejoiced through my pregnancy instead of loathing it. Everyday would have been a day that would have brought me closer to that wonderful blessing and I would have celebrated the whole way through. I wouldn't have almost given up during labor, but I would have pushed harder, focused harder, and tried harder to bring about the end of the situation, if I could have seen the beginning from the end.

Now I know that God is God. He is all knowing, all-powerful and of course He can see the beginning from the end because He already knows the plans for our lives. But we can do that too. We can see situations by looking at the end result. We can already view our husbands as the men that God is going to turn them into and look past all of their faults and shortcomings. Of course I'm not talking about situations of abuse but I am talking about the different situations that we go through with our husbands not being saved. See your husband as that man that God will mold him into being. That man that fulfills your desires (spiritually, emotionally, mentally, and relationally) as a man of God. If you think about that, you will rejoice through the storms and praise God through the tribulations, because the end result will most definitely be worth it.

May 19th

Last night a voice in my head told me that I was not one of God's chosen, and it has been bothering me all day. It was obviously the enemy but for some reason I could not get it out of my head. I told Mark about it and he simply said "So". I responded that it was bugging me and that I knew it wasn't true but I couldn't help but wonder. So he in turn gave me the look. The look that said you are being ridiculous and that you know better than that. He didn't even have to say anything, I just knew it, and I knew that he was right.

About a week ago I saw something in the news that disturbed me also and he (Mark) brought me back to the reality that God was in control. And he always does this. Although I may not talk to Mark about all of the spiritual things going on in my life, I talk to him about everything else. And for someone who is not saved, he always seems to give me a response that would come from someone who is. I have come to the realization that just because he is not saved, does not mean that God is not using him. I am saved and God is looking out for what is best for me. He knows my situation, so He uses the person that I am the most close to get through to me when He needs to. He is already using my husband. My husband is already fulfilling part of God's will for his life and he doesn't even know it.

God Uses our Husbands Too!

G rowth takes time. You may have come out of the world, but that doesn't mean that all of the world has come out of you. It takes time. And with time comes mistakes, doubt, frustrations, and a whole host of other emotions. That's why we are compared to babies at the beginning of our journey with God. With time comes maturity and with maturity comes growth.

My pastor said something one Sunday that really made me think. He said that God gives people gifts, and just because they don't serve Him doesn't mean that He takes their gifts away. Our husbands have gifts, some of which attracted us, and since we are in the will of God and we have certain needs from our husbands, God will use them to give those needs to us if He does not give them to us Himself. He will use our husbands' gifts to fulfill some things that we may have been praying for or to aid us in situations that we need help in. He uses our husbands too and half of the time, they don't even know it.

God loves our husbands just like He loves a man who is serving him. And because we are interceding for them, He is able to work things out in their behalf. Sooner or later they have to recognize that and then it is their choice whether or not to accept it.

My husband recognizes the presence of God in our life. Every once in a while he chalks things up to luck or coincidence but for the most part he knows that God has tremendously blessed us and that every-thing that we have, God has had a hand in it. And every time that God uses him, or blesses us, I know that God's presence surrounds him more and more. Remember, we don't know what's going on inside. God does an inside job and then it starts to show on the outside.

Pray that God uses your husband, and don't doubt that He does. Pray that He uses him in any capacity that he can. Give your husband to Him and watch how He moves.

May 23rd

I didn't go to church today. I didn't go last Tuesday or last Sunday for a host of different reasons or excuses, but today, I didn't go because my husband asked me not to. I was running late. We had a situation with his car that lasted a lot longer than I expected. I tried to get my daughter and I ready as soon as possible but then my husband got into it and told me not to go. I didn't argue, I just listened. Something about it sounded sincere. I can only think of one other time that he asked me not to go, but this was different. I felt like he needed me to stay home. So I did and we talked and talked and laughed and *had one of those beautiful moments in a marriage where it seems like you fall in love all over again.*

It's not just church . . . it's lifestyle

Once my pastor said that it was important for us to be in church. We needed to hear the Word, we needed the fellowship, we needed to bring other people, and God commands us to. But there was a hierarchy that we needed to follow: first God, self, spouse, children, church and then everything else. He said it was important for us to be married to our spouses, and not the church. Now that doesn't mean not to be dedicated to your church, but not so much that you are neglecting your husband, especially if he doesn't come. We need to be wary of that.

I Corinthians 7:34 says that she who is married careth for the things of the world, how she may please her husband. Yes, we are to serve God first. He dwells in the church and the church is his bride. We are to serve Him, and we can do that in and out of the church but our duties at our church should not outweigh our duties of taking care of our husbands. And we have to be careful not to put so much emphasis on our husbands not going to church. We want them to come, I know, but what we really want is a heart change, which will result in a lifestyle change and that is what will prompt them to come to the house of worship and prayer.

When my husband was going to church he was not taking anything in. He was not changing. He was just going because he felt that it was the right thing to do and that it would make me happy. He got no fulfillment out of it. If he wasn't falling asleep then he was daydreaming about the game coming on later that afternoon or of goals that he wanted to accomplish. He rarely paid attention to the Word of God, which made it so easy for him to stop going. Don't get me wrong. If your husband is going to church, continue to encourage it because when that Word goes forth, you never know what is going to be said that could pierce his heart and change his life forever. Romans 10:17 says that faith cometh by hearing, and hearing by the Word of God. This happened to all of us. Something was said that made us change our lives, and in order for that to happen, we had to be in the right place to hear it. I'm just saying don't put so much emphasis on the fact that he is not going to church that it puts a strain on your marriage. You continue to go, you continue to pray, you take every opportunity you can to share your faith with him (and not force it on him) but don't get so freaked out by him not going to church that you neglect him. You are just asking for trouble.

God looks at the heart. He does not keep tally of how many times we went to church. Nor does He do that to our husbands. He is looking for that lifestyle change and commitment to Him and His Word. Let's make sure that our prayers for our husbands do not just include him going to church but we want to pray for that change that will cause him to change his life. That change that will only come by him beginning a relationship with Jesus based on His atoning works on the cross. Coming to church will come but that is not all there is to it. There are people that are faithful church attendees that do not have a relationship with God and therefore are on their way to hell. There are people that may not have a church home but are faithful to God and His Word, saved, baptized, and are on their way to heaven. I know that a good man will not get into heaven lest he be saved (Ephesians 2:8-9) but a good man is a great way to start. Now I am not saying that a good choice for a saved woman is to find a "good man", even if he is not saved. I am speaking to us who are already married to good men who do not serve the Lord. We need to start praying for that great man of ours and think about it before we get so upset about them not going to church. Praise God for the times that they will and let's rejoice in our victory over the situation.

May 25th

I *have wondered what my marriage would be like if my husband was saved, but I just had a thought. How would my marriage be if I were not saved either? Would we be happier? After all, there would be no spiritual struggles, no religious deep conversations, no Sunday struggles and less cares. I wouldn't care if Mark went to church or not, I'd sleep in with him. But on the same token, there would be less self-control, more unforgivness, no account-ability and no spiritual standards. Hmm . . . No thanks, I've already lived that way. And the amazing thing is, I don't miss it, not even for a moment. I have often heard this said, "My best day in the world was worse, than my worst day in Christ". This is true. And even though my husband is not saved, we do not deal with a lot of the situations that I named earlier. I believe that it is God. He has His hand on me and therefore on my husband and my marriage. Mark and I are one. And like I said before, happy. But my best day with him in the world will not compare to my worst day with him in Christ. If I think it's good now, I can't wait until later.*

I Know, I Feel It Too

I t's hard work and it seems like a lot. Every time we go to church or read a chapter in another book it seems like it's something else that we have to do to better ourselves in order to be pleasing in the eyes of God. I know, I feel it too. It's the pressure of doing right and living right and praying and constantly trying to find a balance between the direction that your life is going in vs. the direction that God wants your life to go in. We need to make the right decision and then there's the issue of not knowing which decision is right. It's tough huh? But like my Grandmother has always said to me, "Nobody said it was going to be easy."

Have you ever heard the expression " Only the strong shall survive? " Maybe that's the case here. Maybe our husbands will not except Christ and live for Him because they are not strong enough to be everything that he has called them to be. Maybe in their eyes, they know that they could never live up to that, so why even try.

Mark is a more realistic thinker than I. I believe that I can accomplish everything while Mark understands limitations. What he doesn't understand is that we serve a limitless God. And to put limits on himself is to put limits on God, and God can't function that way and He won't. Once again faith is the key. And if our husbands refuse to believe, then we have to believe for them and you guessed it, pray.

I know that everything in this book comes back to prayer but it's the only way. We have to communicate with God if we want something from Him and if we want to have a relationship with Him. When is the last time you received something that you really wanted without asking? It doesn't happen often. And when it does happen it's because a need is recognized and remembered. We need to remember our husbands on so many levels when we pray and this is one of them. We need to recognize their needs and pray for them. The hardest thing is making sure we are praying for husbands' needs, and not just ours.

You know, sometimes our husbands need things that we don't, and we don't know about. Pray for God to give your husband everything that he needs to have a strong relationship with Him. Pray that God reveals to you the things that you can do to help and then do it, even if you don't want to. Don't think of it as if you are doing this for your husband as much as you think of it as you are doing what God wants you to do and then it may not seem like so much. We are human. And I know that as a working mom and wife it seems as though I have more than enough to do already. And to add something else that I need to work on seems like another thing that I have to add to my "To Do List." I feel like I don't have enough time to work on the things that I need to improve myself, let alone working on myself to improve my husband. But when you put God in it, it changes things. When I think about all that God has, is, and has yet to do in my life, I am willing to do anything for Him. And then it doesn't seem like so much and if it still does, ask God to help you balance things. Ask Him to put you on a schedule and when things come up, ask Him to remind you of things that you are trying to change in your life so that you can make all of the progress that you need.

May 26ᵗʰ

Today was a cool day. I learned so much. To God be the glory. First of all, I really experienced what God is talking about when He says our tongue is powerful. Yesterday was not a great day for me, but what I realized is that I confessed it early on. I told a friend of mine that I was having a bad day and sure enough I did. I didn't really think about it until today. This morning things were not going my way and I decided that I was going to have a great day. I confessed it and minute-by-minute, it became that way. As I enjoyed what my words created I learned something else. I learned how to really truly believe in me. I get so tired of saying I am going to do things and never doing them. I do that a lot when it comes to things like losing weight, saving money, writing a book, and for some reason I allow things and circumstances to get in my way. I'm not doing that anymore. I just got tired of being tired. And today, I actually believed in me. I did everything that I said I was going to and I have to continue to do it everyday. And with God's help, I'm going to be okay, I know I am and so is my husband. See, God spoke to me today and gave me a new outlook. He fired me up and showed me how awesome He truly is. I can't go back, I won't. I have faith in His Word, and since I have confessed it, I know now more than I ever have before. God is faithful and He is all I'll ever need. If He said that something is to be, it's to be. satan doesn't stand a chance. My husband will be set free.

God's Will

God's will . . . hmmm. It used to be scary to me. I thought about it selfishly. I thought, what if God's will is not my will. Then what would I do? What if He didn't have the same goals for me as I had for myself? What if His will wasn't for me to be with Mark, or wasn't for me to be married? His will was going to prevail but what if I didn't like it? Was there anyway I could change His mind? Selfish, faithless and blind, that was me. It wasn't until I accepted the fact that God's will was greater than anything that I could imagine for my life that I lost that fear. Why would I want anything else? He is

all knowing, all mighty, and supernatural. And I am
. . . human, absolutely nothing compared to Him.

Even though we are nothing compared to Him,
we mean everything to Him. So much so that He
took the time to devise a plan for each and every one
of us. Within those plans, lays His will for our lives.
What do we have to fear? Jeremiah 29:11 says, *"For
I know the thoughts that I think toward you, saith the
Lord, thoughts of peace, and not of evil, to give you
an expected end."* He has thoughts of peace towards
us and wants our lives to come to an expected end.
Heaven. That's how we expect our lives to end, right?
That's what's promised to us if we accept Christ for
our Lord and Savior, confess our sins, and live for
Him. Contrary to popular belief, He does not just
have a will for the lives of *His people*, but He also
has plans for those who don't follow Him, or maybe
just aren't following Him right now. He has something for them too, including the men in our lives.

God knows everything. Therefore He bases His decisions on the things that He knows. We don't know anything (compared to Him) so we base our decisions on what we don't know, which doesn't do anything but cause us to make decisions blindly, and that's not very smart. God knew that our husband's were not going to be saved at this point and time in our lives. And He knew that we would struggle with it. But He also knew how much stronger this would make us, and how much closer this would make us to Him. (With all the praying and everything!) For some reason we need to go through this and when it is all over we will understand. But until that time we need to have faith that God ultimately has his best interest in mind, which is in our best interest too. It's hard to let go of control like that but remember, we belong to Him . . . He does not belong to us.

I heard it put like this once and it made total sense to me. God has bought us for a price. He paid for us by sacrificing His son so He could forgive our sins. That means He owns us. Our life does not belong to us; it belongs to Him (I Corinthians 6:20). In the whole scheme of things it really doesn't matter if we like what is going on or not. It is not up to us. But fortunately for us our Owner is a gentleman and He does care. He want us to be happy as well as fulfill His purpose for our lives so He invented prayer. It is an avenue that we can take to express to Him our hurts, doubts, fears, and desires. Then He makes decisions based on His infinite wisdom. In the end it's God will that really matters and we have to be vessels willing to be used.

God please use me as a vessel to bring my husband to you. Tell me the words to say, and not to say. Open his heart so that he has room enough to receive it. Help me to be patient, and loving throughout the whole process. Give me the strength not to get frustrated and the wisdom to stick through it all. I thank you God for caring enough about me to forgive my sins and blessing me with the opportunity to serve you. I thank you for your will being done. In Jesus name I pray, Amen.

May 29ᵗʰ

I struggled all day with an issue. One that I shouldn't even have to think about. Especially after God told me that my husband was watching me and that my actions spoke volumes. I was still debating on whether or not I was going to church. It is Friday, and I am tired, and I am definitely going on Sunday, and so and so is not going and . . . and . . . excuse after excuse I gave until the Holy Spirit told me that I don't serve God out of convenience. I serve Him because He has called me, because I love Him, and because that is what He has told me to do. Needless to say I went, but not because I wanted my *husband to see me and follow my lead, but because that is what God told me to do. As much as I want my husband to be saved, I was not willing to give up my Friday night to do it. Not for that cause. But for the cause that I live my life for, I am willing to do anything. And to me, that speaks volumes.*

Because God said so

I ask God for lots of stuff. I do. I pray for everything. He is my daddy, and that's what little girls do. They ask their father for lots of things as do I. That doesn't mean that I get everything that I ask for, but the things that I do get, I get because God says so. God says lots of things in his Word. I don't know about you, but I have trouble consistently reading it. It's something that I am definitely going to work on. If we knew everything that God said it would be much easier, you would think. But even the things that we know that God says, we have a hard time truly believing it. Why is that? When our pastor

187

gets up there and talks about the promises of God we will shout amen and hallelujah but go home and worry, disregarding everything that God says. It's not that we don't know it, we just don't believe it, even though we say we do.

When Mark and I first starting tithing I had trouble with it. I didn't have trouble with the issue of giving but I always seem to run out of money before I completed the process. Being a teacher I only get paid once a month and Mark gets paid twice. So I tried to split up the money four ways so that I would have something to give every month. By the time of the end of month came, I was always out of money therefore unable to pay the rest of my tithes. I asked my pastor how I should handle it. He told me that the Bible said that we should give the first fruits of our labor as our tithe. (Nehemiah 10:37) That means that your tithe should be the first thing that you pay. For some reason it was hard for me to give all of that money at once. It seemed so much smaller when I divided it by four. But then my pastor said something very interesting to me. He said that it seemed that I didn't believe that I would get back what I gave like it says we would in the Bible. I didn't think that was it but it did make sense. If I truly believed that I was going to get everything back then I would just give it all when I needed to instead of breaking it up. Does that make sense? I should have just done what God had told me to, regardless of when I wanted to pay it because He already said that I'd receive it back pressed down, shaken together and running over. (Luke 6:38) It's kind of like fear. What is the point of being afraid of anything if we believe what God says about protecting us? But for some reason we still become afraid. What is the deal?

Don't you ever get tired of the same old same old? Going to sleep and waking up the same. God tells us to do this, and tells us that He will do that

189

and imagine how much better off we would be if we just listen to Him because He says so. We know that we can trust him so what is it with the apprehension? We need to change because God says so. God says that we are to have faith in Him. He gives us several examples in the Bible of people that are going through with undying faith and just when it seems that they can not last another minute, God comes through.

Let's change. Let's do it together. Chances are that when you are reading this I will still need prayers for several areas of my life that I will be trying to change. So let us pray one for another. I'll pray for you and you'll pray for me and together let's change. Let's change into true believers. Not just believers in Christ, but **real** believers in His Word. It's not just our husbands who need the changing. It's us too. If it wasn't then you wouldn't need to read this book and I wouldn't need to write it. We'd just know.

June 3rd

*L*ast night, I couldn't sleep. I woke up several times. Each time I just turned my attention to God and thought about the previous day. I was thinking about the church service and how the pastor was talking about how God answers prayers when you are in His will. This made me think. If I am out of the will of God, and doing all of this praying for my husband, then I am doing it for nothing. I wasn't sure if I was in the will of God for every area of my life. I still have things that I struggle with. I know that I don't have to be perfect but I do have to be better. I *have to be actively seeking God and His will for my life, and not just praying for my husband.*

True Prayer

❖

James 5:16 . . . The effectual, fervent prayer

of a righteous man availeth much.

S ometimes, a Bible verse brings greater understanding when it is broken down and applied
to our lives. Let's take a look at this scripture and
focus on a few key words.

Effectual: Effectual in the Hebrew means to be
operative, be at work, to put forth power. So first, our
prayers must be real and not just for show. They have
to be of value, of sustenance, worth something to us
and worth something to God. Then we have to put

our prayers to work. We have to make them operative and make them work by putting forth power. By using the power of faith and prayer we are showing God that our husbands' salvation means something to us, and that we believe that our God can do anything, including saving them.

Fervent: Fervent in the Hebrew means to be active, efficient and mighty in. James 2:20 says that faith without works is dead. So we have to be active in our prayers and exercise it by calling things that are not, as though they are and we have to be efficient in it. Efficient means to be working productively with minimum wasted effort or expense. Let's not waste time or effort. Let's pray and exercise faith until it is done, not ceasing. Several synonyms for the word fervent are fanatical, burning, eager, and enthusiastic. Wow. Fanatical and burning are powerful images. If you are fanatical about something, you are crazy about it. You will do anything to get what you want.

In our case fanatical might be praying often for it, crying out for it, fasting for it, throwing ourselves on the altar for it without ceasing until we get it. Burning for something is that unyielding desire that will not go away until you receive what you are waiting for. Do you have that kind of desire in your heart for your husband's salvation? Do you go to any and every length possible for this cause? I know I haven't, and inside I really want to. I tell myself I need to fast and I need to go to the altar. Sometimes it's the faces that get in my way. You know, the people in your church who might think you're crazy for going up to the altar every opportunity you get. You would do it to save someone's life wouldn't you? Isn't saving your husband's life worth it?

Righteous: Righteous means so many things, but in the Hebrew it means keeping the commands of God. The dictionary definition breaks those commands down. Let's take a look: Virtuous, moral, good, just, blameless, upright, honorable, honest, respectable, and decent. Now look at the antonym: sinful. These definitions say so much. Perfect is not in the definition because there is only one perfect person, Jesus Christ, but there are many righteous men. It's in the striving to be like Jesus by keeping God's commands that we become righteous, and in that righteousness our prayers avail.

Availeth: Availeth in the Hebrew means to be serviceable for good, to have power, to exert, wield, and have strength to overcome. Synonyms for this word are help, benefits, to be strong or to be of value or gain.

Now let's put this verse together again. Here's one way: An operative, fanatic prayer of a good man, wields much. Let's do another one. A powerful, burning prayer of an honorable man, has the strength to overcome much. One more. A working, eager prayer of a just man, gains much. Get the picture.

So in order for us to gain from our prayers for our husbands they must be effectual and fervent, and we must be righteous.

Part Two

"If my people, who are called by my Name,

will humble themselves and pray and seek My

face and turn from their wicked ways, then

will I hear from heaven and will forgive their

sin and will heal their land." 2 Chronicles

7:14

Listen, this is very important, so please pay close attention. I think that a lot of us miss this verse, but my pastor makes sure that we don't.

He goes over it a lot and applies it to a lot of different sermons and I think that it is relative to us too. Not just for our situation, for our lives. But since the focus of this book is how we deal with and get the victory in dealing with our unsaved husband, that's the perspective that I am going to come from and then you can take this and apply it to your entire life. First let's start with "If my people, who are called by my name" . . . now I am not assuming that everyone that is reading this book is "sure nuff" saved. You know the difference. Not the ones who say that they are saved but live like hell. I am talking about the people who know that if they died at this very moment, they are 100% sure that they would go to heaven. I am talking about those of us who love God, serve God, live for God, have accepted Jesus as our personal lord and savior, and believe that Jesus Christ died, was buried, and rose on the third day for the resurrection of our sins "sure nuff" saved. Another part of that is that God considers His "people" to be His daughters and sons, and once we accept Him as our Father, we are just that. And then there is this "called by His Name" stuff. To be called is to be proclaimed, to be named . . . but not just anything. We are called by God's Name. The word called there is "quara" in Hebrew which means to call out, invite, preach and proclaim. We are proclaimed to be God's people. The next step is to humble ourselves. My pastor gave a great example about what the world considers to be humble. He said that if a football player makes a touch down and drops the ball without all of the celebration then everyone says what a humble guy he is when in fact we really do not know. We don't know this person's lifestyle, we just saw an action. To be humble means to be brought into subjection, to be low and to be under and in this case, to be under God.

After we are humble then we need to pray and seek God's face. We need to seek his presence. Now how do we do that? How do we seek God's presence? We can ask Him for it through prayer, we can find it through studying His Word, we can fast and go to a church that teaches His Word. We can stop going after our own agenda and start seeking out God's agenda. The Bible says that if we draw near to God, that He will draw near to us. (James 4:8) We need to desire that relationship with Him and go after it in every way we know. Matthew 7:7 says to ask and it shall be given you; seek, and you shall find; knock, and it shall be opened unto you.

In conjunction with seeking God we also need to turn from our wicked ways. To repent for our sins and to turn away from them. After we have done all of that then God will hear from heaven and heal our land. When I first read this scripture I thought that God would hear from Heaven . . . and just that . . . I literally thought that He would just hear. But the word hear there means much more than that. That word is "shama" in the Hebrew and it literally means that God will not just hear but He will hear with attention and interest. He will actually listen to us. God will listen in order to give or not give His consent but He will listen. Sometimes I just hear my daughter but I do not comprehend what she is saying because I am not listening. The Bible says that after we do what He has asked us to do in this scripture that He will actually listen to us. Psalm 66:18 says that if we regard iniquity in our hearts that the Lord will not hear us. I believe that there are a lot of people out there who pray, and they just pray their little hearts out and nothing ever changes and then they question God. Whether they become angry with Him, just flat our stop believing in Him, or think that He has forgotten them, they turn their backs on Him and blame Him for their faults. If this is you, or even if it is not you I challenge you to weigh your lifestyle against every-thing that these scriptures say and then ask yourself if God hears you, or if He is truly listening. It is not too late to start doing what it takes for God to heal our land, our lives, and to answer our prayers.

June 6th

*G*od is really moving in our lives. He told my husband something a couple of days ago that seems to be manifesting now. And the best part about it is that he recognized that it was God. He has also made a huge decision for our family that I was not 100% behind but I decided that I was going to trust in his faith and now, everything is falling in place for that too. I **am** married to a mighty man of God. A man that has the heart to listen to God's words. That is powerful. All of this time that I have been writing this book, I have been married to **this** man. I am not saying that my prayers did not help, I am sure they *did. But I can't help to think that maybe I have had blinders on all this time. Maybe he has always been and because he didn't act the way that I thought he should act, I deemed him not something that he always was. We are who God calls us to be. No matter what the world thinks of us, no matter what we think of us and in this case, no matter what our spouse thinks of us, but I have learned my lesson. God has answered my prayers. I don't care what anybody thinks. He is who he is . . . a mighty, powerful man of God. He **will** eventually walk in it. And you know what, he's mine.*

Just Listen

❖

What can I say? This book is not ending the way that I expected it to either. I expected for me to write a chapter about when my husband gave his life to God. One in which he runs up to the altar and cries out to God. One filled with drama and suspense and ultimately, victory. One that would send shivers down your spine. But I am not writing the chapters in my husband's life, God is, and the above scenario hasn't happened yet, if it will happen at all. Don't get me wrong. I know my husband will be completely saved but it may happen in a more subtle way. It really doesn't matter though because the changes are already taking place and have been for a while. I just didn't see it. Not only do I see it now, but I feel it . . . I feel it so much so that I already know the title for the sequel to this book, <u>Help, I'm married to a Godly Man</u>! Ladies, please don't think that there are not trials and tribulations in that situation too. It's just another journey that we will go through together in our quest for being the women and wives that God has called us to be.

But before we get there, let's recap all of the things that God has taught us, therefore if you are ever in a situation when you need a quick review, this chapter will suffice.

1. You need a relationship with God, through faith in Jesus Christ, to be saved. That's everyone, our husbands too! That is what the Word says therefore it is truth. (Roman 10: 9-10)

2. For as a man thinketh in his heart, so is he. (Proverbs 23:7a) If we think negatively about our

marriages, then they will become a reflection of our thought life. Be careful of what you think, even when you become frustrated and discouraged. You have to know that God's will *will* be done. On that same note we need to watch what we say. Negative words breathe negative consequences. Let's confess the positive and watch God work.

3. Pray – need I say more? It works. Not only that, but your relationship with God becomes more fruitful and more intimate. Prayer opens doors for us and covers us and our husbands. Especially when they are not living a godly life. Our intercessing may be the only thing that causes a change in their heart and in their life. Never give up, God hears your prayers.

4. Never give up . . . I know it feels like it's never going to happen. That he will never be saved, that it is impossible. But we must stay strong

and continue to believe. Our husbands' souls are important to us. And we have to be willing to fight for them always, no matter how long it takes.

5. He is not holding you back . . . you are. Remember, if you need a man in order for you to do God's will then there is something wrong. You should be able to do God's will with or without your husband's blessing. And I am not saying that this is going to be easy. God's perfect will is we (Christians) marry Christians only. 2 Corinthians 6:14 says "Be ye not yoked together with unbelievers: for what fellowship hath righteousness with unrighteousness? And what communion hath light with darkness?" We **are** supposed to be equally yoked and that is what we are praying for but since we are not right now, we need to repent to God for that sin in order to make things right with Him. I Corinthians 7:34 says that she that is married careth for the things of the world, *how she may*

please her husband. So as we already know, it will be difficult to follow and fulfill God's will when the person that we are made one with, our husbands, are not saved. Our relationship with God depends solely on us. Pray and watch him work.

6. Answer his questions the best you can. And if you can not, go to someone who can. It is important that we show our husbands that their questions about God are important and that we get them the correct answers. We are their closest connection to the things of God and we need to make their questions a priority.

7. Romans 3:23 says that we are all sinners and fall short of the glory of God. No one is perfect. We must not judge our husbands for their shortcomings and their sins because we do it too, or have done it. Our husbands must feel comfortable and not threatened. They have to know that Jesus did

not come back for the perfect but for the sinners and that we all have fallen short but God's grace and mercy extends to all of us. (Just look at the character of the people that Jesus hung out with).

8. It's about lifestyle . . . not just theirs, but ours too. Remember they are watching us. If we are doing something ungodly then we are sending the message to them that they can do that also and still be in the kingdom. Going to church is important, but let's not completely lose our minds over it. It is lifestyle. And we want our husbands to change their lives and consistently going to church will come.

9. Last but certainly not least is the reality that no matter what, it's God's will. If He wants it to happen, it will. That phrase "Let go and let God" is true. Continue praying for your husband. Speak truth into his life. Do God's will within your marriage and let Him do the rest. Allow God to

handle this situation while you keep your eyes fixated on Him. He will see your obedience and make the best choice for your life.

A very wise woman once spoke at marriage seminar and she said, "Instead of spending all of your time with your mouth to the ear of God, try putting your ear to the mouth of God and just listen." Throughout your life, not just your married life, but your whole life, take the time to just listen to God. He will guide you through everything.

Every night before I wrote in this book I prayed for God to tell me what He wanted me to tell His people and every night I just listened. I listened, typed, and was amazed at the things that God wanted to tell His wives whose husbands may not have been in His will. He taught me first and told me to bring it to you in the form of this book. Listening to God is one of best things that I have learned throughout this process. Doing His will is another. Having that faith, that unmovable, unshakable faith that my prayers, that wonderful language of love and praise, will and have been answered.

Our husbands are saved. Not only are they saved but they are powerful men of God. We need to confess this always. No matter what it looks like on the outside, God works on the inside and He is chipping away all that mess that is holding our husbands back. Continue to strive to be the best wife you can be, stay encouraged, listen to God, pray and confess your blessings. Thank you so much for taking this journey with me. I pray for your husbands' salvation and for a more fruitful marriage that results in a blessed, Godly relationship. In Jesus Christ's Holy Name, Amen.

Author Biography

Clarissa Lee Kennerly was born in Winchester, Virginia. At an early age she knew that God had called her to write. She started off with poetry and the beginnings of several fiction novels until she realized that she was called to write more compelling and personal novels about her issues, struggles, and victories over them through Christ Jesus. She married her high school sweetheart in June of 2000. Since then, God has blessed them with two beautiful children.

CPSIA information can be obtained at www.ICGtesting.com
Printed in the USA
LVOW131520200412

278498LV00001BA/45/P

9 781604 774634